DRACULA IS A PAIN IN THE NECK

DRACULA
Is a Pain in the Neck

by Elizabeth Levy
illustrated by
Mordicai Gerstein

A TARGET BOOK
published by
the Paperback Division of
W.H. Allen & Co. Plc

A Target Book
Published in 1986
by the Paperback Division of
W.H. Allen & Co. PLC
44 Hill Street, London W1X 8LB

First published in the United States of America by
Harper & Row, 1983

Text Copyright © Elizabeth Levy, 1983
Illustrations copyright © Mordicai Gerstein, 1983

Printed and bound in Great Britain by
Anchor Brendon Limited, Tiptree, Essex

ISBN 0 426 20249 X

*to David Harris, who asked if Dracula was a Boy
Scout*

CONTENTS

Dracula's Pillow

"Only a baby would take that stupid pillow to camp," Sam said. Sam and Robert were packing to go to camp for the month of August. Sam had gone last year, but this would be Robert's first time at sleep-away camp.

Robert looked at the small frayed pillow he had slept with ever since he was a baby in a crib. Then he saw his Dracula doll sitting on his desk. It was missing one fang and one arm. He glanced back at his pillow. Suddenly he had an idea.

"I'm not taking my pillow for me. I'm taking it for Dracula. Dracula always sleeps on it. Dracula won't want to come to camp without my pillow . . . *his* pillow." Carefully, Robert placed Dracula on the pillow.

"Oh boy," groaned Sam. "You're not just taking a pillow, you're taking your doll too."

"Dracula is *not* a doll," protested Robert. "He's the king of all vampires, half man, half bat. He lives at night, and he drinks people's blood. In fact, he's about to drink your blood."

Robert waved his doll at Sam. Sam pushed him away, and before they knew it they were shoving each other back and forth across the room and screaming.

Their mother ran into the room. "What's going on?" she demanded.

"Dracula attacked Sam," said Robert, giggling. "He doesn't like him at all."

"Robert's going to take this stupid pillow to camp. Everyone's going to know my brother is a baby," said Sam.

"Sam, leave Robert alone," warned their mother.

"He started it," protested Sam. "He's going to make me feel like a dodo. Tell him he can't take his baby pillow."

"It's not a baby pillow. It's Dracula's pillow," said Robert. "Dracula does what he wants to do, and he wants to take his pillow to camp."

Mrs. Bamford sighed. "Sam, you know this is Robert's first year at overnight camp, and if he wants to take his pillow it's not really your business. Besides, he's only just over the chicken pox, and if he wants his pillow, it's fine."

"IT'S NOT MY PILLOW. IT'S DRACU-LA'S," yelled Robert. "I'M NOT TAKING IT FOR ME. IT'S FOR HIM."

"Have it your own way," said Mrs. Bamford. "Just stop screaming."

"Baby," muttered Sam into Robert's ear so softly that Mrs. Bamford couldn't hear.

Mrs. Bamford drove Sam and Robert to the bus station. Dracula and his pillow were packed in Robert's knapsack. "Hiya, Samson, how's it going," shouted Billy, Sam's best friend from last year. Soon Sam was surrounded by old friends.

Robert held on to his mother's hand. She squeezed it. "You're going to have a wonderful time," she said.

"Right," said Robert, swallowing hard, watching his brother talking with his friends. He noticed a tall thin man looking at him. The man walked over and held out his hand.

"Is this little Robert?" asked the man. Robert took his hand and tried not to wince as the man pumped it.

"I'm not little," said Robert. "I'm seven years old and my height is average for my age. Well, maybe just an inch below average."

The man smiled at Mrs. Bamford. "I only meant little compared to me. I'm your head counselor. My name is Robert, too. You can call me Big Robert."

Robert smiled weakly.

"Do you want to see how big and strong you'll be by the end of the summer?" Before Robert could answer, Big Robert rolled up his sleeves and the muscles on his arms bobbed up and down like kids on a trampoline.

Robert didn't know what to say. Neither did his mother.

"Everyone from the counselors to our littlest campers will be this strong by the end of the summer," said Big Robert. "Now it's time to say good-bye to your mother and join the other campers."

Robert gave his mother a big hug.

"It's only for four weeks," she said as she kissed him.

"That's six hundred and seventy-two hours," said Robert.

Sam left his friends and hugged his mother too. Then he took Robert's hand and led him onto the bus. "I was scared last year too," whispered Sam, and at that moment Robert was glad they were going to the same camp.

2

Skinny Vampires

The bus drive to camp took four hours, and Robert spent most of it praying that he wouldn't get carsick. A boy named Jared got sick, and the bus had to stop twice for him. Jared looked very green by the time they arrived.

Sam took Robert to his tent. "See ya later, alligator," he said, and then he was gone. There were three other kids in the tent, including Jared. The other two kids were named Matthew and Alex. Matthew was tall with curly brown hair. Alex was fairly tall too, only he was pretty fat.

They knew they were the youngest kids in camp and they all asked each other their birthdays. Robert was happy to find out that he wasn't the youngest camper. Jared was three months younger than anybody else.

Robert unpacked his pillow and put it on his cot. He loved the feel of his pillow's soft cotton—almost as soft as his mother's kisses when she tucked him in at night.

"What's that?" asked Jared, who was sleeping next to him.

"Uh, it's nothing," said Robert.

"It looks like a baby pillow," said Jared. "Hey, kids, look what Robert Bamford is going to sleep with."

The other kids in the tent scrambled over the cots to see what was on Robert's bed. At that moment Robert knew that he should have listened to his brother and left his pillow at home.

"This is not a baby pillow," said Robert. "It is Dracula's bed. If anyone touches it, Dracula will bite him." Carefully, Robert took out his Dracula doll and placed it on his pillow.

"That's a neat doll," said Jared.

"He's not a doll." Robert paused. "This is really Dracula. He is a vampire who drinks people's blood. If he drinks your blood, then you become a vampire too."

Just then a red-haired man stumbled into their tent. He looked about eighteen, and his T-shirt was soaked through with sweat. It clung to his stomach, which was quite large.

"I'm George, your counselor," gasped the man as he flung himself onto an empty cot. "I'm sorry I'm late, but Big Robert grabbed me and made me do a hundred push-ups. Give me a chance to catch my breath, and then I'll catch all your names."

"You won't have trouble remembering one of our names," said Alex. "Dracula!"

"Yeah," said Matthew. "We just found out that Dracula is bunking in our tent. He's even got his own pillow."

Matthew grabbed Dracula and the pillow and waved them high in the air to show George.

"Give that back to me," shouted Robert.

Alex threw Dracula and the pillow at George. "It looks like Dracula has been in some battles," said George, pointing to Dracula's missing fang and missing arm.

"He has, but he always wins," said Robert. "He's a killer."

"I'll tell you what," said George, handing Dracula back to Robert, but keeping the pillow. "Let's forget about Dracula for a while. We have a lot to go over before dinner. Tonight, at bedtime, I'll tell you a story about Dracula."

"Will you give me back my pillow?"

asked Robert, hoping he didn't sound as if he were begging. "I mean, Dracula's pillow," he added quickly.

George examined the pillow.

"What are you looking for?" asked Robert.

"Drops of blood," intoned George. Then he grinned and handed the pillow back to Robert.

The first day of camp went by in a whirl. Robert felt there were more new rules to learn than at school. He hardly saw Sam at all. After dinner they sang songs, and then Big Robert sent the youngest tent to bed. None of them liked having to go to sleep earlier than everyone else.

Robert crawled into his cot. He had never slept in a tent before, and the moon made strange shadows on the canvas over his head. Robert was used to the sounds of the city, but the high-pitched sounds of the crickets were so loud he didn't think he'd ever sleep. He lay on his stomach and tucked his pillow under his chest. A cold wind blew through the tent. Robert shivered.

"Tell us the Dracula story," demanded Matthew.

"Ah, Dracula, the most famous vampire of them all," said George in a spooky voice. "Dracula is a count who was born long ago, but he still lives. He cannot be killed. Strange that you should all be talking about him. Dracula has a taste for young blood, and you know we are the youngest tent."

Robert hugged his pillow even tighter.

George continued. "Dracula and other vampires don't need food, but they need blood every night. If a vampire bites you, then you wake up with a craving for blood, and you bite another person, and soon you are a vampire too."

George's voice drifted off.

"What should we do if we're attacked by a vampire?" asked Alex.

"Wave garlic in its face," said George. "Vampires hate real food. In fact, vampires are always skinny, too skinny. Dracula could

easily pass for a marathon runner. He moves among us, and nobody knows who he is. He could easily be a camper." George laughed to himself. "Many people have asked the question, 'Does Dracula go to summer camp?' but nobody has lived to find the answer."

3

Teeth Marks

The next morning was cold and dreary, but Big Robert had scheduled an eight A.M. swim, so George took them down to the lake. The air was even colder than the water, and mist, looking like dancing ghosts, rose from the lake.

They got undressed in a spindly cabin with cobwebs in the corner. Robert was the palest person there. Jared, of course, was the blackest. But Matthew and Alex had nice healthy summer tans.

Robert peeled off his sweat shirt. He wished that he hadn't had chicken pox all July. He knew he looked pale, and he had lost weight while he was sick, too. Robert was normally thin. Now his arms looked like chicken wings. He felt as if everyone was staring at him. He put on his bathing suit and turned around.

Everyone *was* staring at him.

"Why are you so pale?" asked Jared.

Before Robert could answer, Matthew answered for him. "I bet he didn't get enough blood to drink last night." Suddenly Matthew pointed his finger at Robert's neck. "Do you see what I see?" he demanded.

Automatically, Robert put his hand up to his neck. He felt two chicken-pox scabs that hadn't fallen off yet.

"Ah ha!" shouted Alex. "He's hiding something." Alex jumped on Robert and tried to pull his hands away from his neck.

Robert tried to fight Alex off, but Alex grabbed his wrists.

"Leave me alone," cried Robert.

"That's what vampires always say," shouted Matthew, urging Alex on. The other kids gathered around. Slowly Alex forced Robert's hands down from his neck.

Everyone gasped when they saw two little red marks on his neck. "Teeth marks," cried Alex.

"Dracula's been drinking his blood," whispered Matthew.

Jared stared at Robert.

"It's just chicken pox," protested Robert.

"Now Robert is a vampire too," said Matthew. "He brought Dracula into our tent, and now they're going to turn all of us into vampires."

"I am *not* a vampire," stammered Robert, close to tears. He rubbed his neck.

Just then George poked his head into the changing room. "Come on, boys," he said. "Time for your swim."

Luckily, Robert was an excellent swimmer. He jumped into the lake, and swam as fast as he could. George called the head counselor over to watch Robert swim.

"Robert Bamford, you have an excellent crawl stroke," said Big Robert.

"Wait till you see him fly," said Matthew.

"No, he only does that at night," said Alex.

Robert swam to the float. He pulled himself up. He was shivering. He looked across the lake and wished that he was somewhere

far, far away. Suddenly he heard someone climb onto the raft.

"Oh, no, Dracula," said the voice.

Robert turned around. It was Jared with Billy, Sam's best friend.

"Dracula?" asked Billy.

"Yeah, Dracula," said Jared, climbing onto the raft. "Robert Bamford is Dracula."

Billy looked as if he thought they were just little kids fooling around. "Do you know why vampires are unpopular?" he asked.

"No," said Jared.

"Because they're a pain in the neck," said Billy. He laughed very hard.

"That's not so funny," muttered Jared.

"You're right," said Billy. "I'd better not make jokes. Dracula might pick on *me* next." Billy pantomimed being scared to death of Robert.

"Forget it," said Robert. He did a quick racing dive, his body cutting through the cool water like a knife. He started to cry, but because he was already in the water, no one could see his tears.

Camp Hunter Creek was a small camp, only fifty boys and fifteen counselors. Rumors that Robert was a vampire spread from tent to tent quicker than asteroid flashes on a video game.

After lunch, Sam cornered Robert outside the dining room. "What's going on?" he demanded. "Everyone's calling me Dracula's brother."

"I hate it here," said Robert. "I'm thinking of running away."

"Running away never solves anything," said Sam. "Remember, that's what Mom always says."

"Wait until people start calling her Dracula's mom," said Robert. "She'll think of running away too."

"Promise me you won't run away," said Sam anxiously.

Robert didn't answer. Instead he looked thoughtful. "Do you think the real Dracula is mad at me because I lied about my pillow?" asked Robert.

Sam stared at his younger brother as if he had gone bonkers. "What are you talking about?"

"I lied to you and told you that my pillow was Dracula's pillow. That was the only way I could bring it without you calling me a baby. But suppose Dracula is real, and he can see and hear everything? Then he would be mad at me. Maybe he's the one who is making everyone think I'm a vampire."

Sam shook his head. "I think you've been in the sun too long. Your brains are turning to mush. Forget about Dracula and your pillow. Your only mistake was bringing them in the first place. Just promise me you won't run away."

"I promise," said Robert, since he knew he was too scared to run away without Sam. Maybe if things got too tough, he and Sam could run away together.

4

I Want to Bury Dracula

Somehow Robert managed to get through the day. He had a free hour before bedtime. Robert wanted to just forget about his troubles and read a book. He went back to his tent. Jared was alone, lying on his bed, reading a book too.

Robert plopped down on his bed. He looked at his Dracula doll. "You don't know the trouble you're causing," sighed Robert.

"Does Dracula talk to you?" whispered Jared.

"Yeah," said Robert sarcastically. "Do you know the best way to talk to a vampire?"

Jared shook his head.

"Long distance," said Robert. "I heard that joke at lunch."

"But I wasn't asking as a joke," said Jared. "I want to know. Can you really talk to Dracula?"

"He's just a doll. . . ."

"I thought so," said Jared.

"I'll never survive a month here," said Robert. "Today was the worst day of my life."

"I believe you," said Jared. "I don't love it. First I get carsick, and then I find out I'm the youngest. I'm sorry I started teasing you about your pillow and Dracula. I don't know what made me do it." Jared laughed nervously. "Maybe Dracula made me do it."

Robert stared at the Dracula doll in his hand. He could hear Sam's voice saying, "Your only mistake was bringing that stupid doll and pillow."

"Maybe the real Dracula is here in camp, after all," said Robert softly.

"Huh?" exclaimed Jared.

"Maybe he's like a ghost who sees and hears everything, and he hates me because I put him on my baby pillow."

"Yeah," said Jared. "Like I have an uncle who hates it when I play with my superhero dolls. He says it's sissy. My father tells him to leave me alone."

"Yeah, sort of like that. . . . Suppose the real Dracula doesn't like it they've made plastic dolls of him. . . . He could be mad at me because I bought one, and he's making everyone tease me."

"The real Dracula . . ." repeated Jared. "He was born long ago."

"Maybe he hates plastic," said Robert. "My mom hates plastic. She says the world is getting to be buried in plastic."

Jared nodded.

"Buried . . . I wish Dracula were buried," said Robert. "Hey, that's not a bad idea. Maybe if we buried my plastic doll, the real Dracula would be happy and he'd stop haunting me or whatever he's doing."

"You want to bury Dracula?" asked Jared incredulously.

Robert nodded. "I think I have to. Will you help me?"

Jared shuddered. "I guess so," he whispered.

"I don't want any of the other kids to know I'm doing this," said Robert.

Jared looked at his watch. "Taps will be in about fifteen minutes," he said. "Want to do it now?"

Robert nodded. They took his flashlight. As they left the tent, they saw Alex and Matthew coming up the path, giggling. Robert and Jared ignored them. Outside, the sun was just setting, and the pine trees made huge

shadows on the ground. They ran to a se-
cluded circle of trees just above the tents.
Robert placed Dracula on the ground and
picked up a sharp-pointed stick. He dug
through the pine cones and pine needles,
down into the soft dark dirt below. Jared
found a sharp stone and helped him. Finally,
they had a hole about six inches long and
three inches deep.

Solemnly, Robert placed Dracula in it.

"Aren't you going to say anything?"
asked Jared.

Robert thought for a moment. "O Dracula, may you sleep for a thousand years, and
I am sorry I made fun of you."

"Me too," said Jared.

In the distance, they could hear the bu-
gler play taps. "Day is done . . . gone the
sun . . ." The mournful tune echoed
through the camp.

"We'd better hurry," whispered Jared.

Quickly Robert piled dirt and pine needles over Dracula. As the last strains of taps
filled the air, no trace of Dracula remained.

5

The Coning of Beds

When they got back to the tent, Alex and Matthew were already in bed. "Where have you two been?" demanded Alex.

"Uh, nowhere," stammered Robert.

Robert crawled into bed. He screamed. His bed was full of pine cones and pine needles. "Oh, no," he groaned. He looked around for George, but George wasn't there. Alex and Matthew sat up in bed, laughing. They bombarded Robert with pine cones.

"Leave me alone," yelled Robert.

Alex and Matthew just laughed. Jared didn't laugh, but he didn't come to Robert's defense either. Robert forced himself not to cry. He took the sheets off his bed and carried them outside, trying to walk as tall as he could. He wished that George was there to yell at Alex and Matthew.

Robert stood outside all by himself and waved his sheet in the air, covering himself with prickly pine needles. He looked up at the hill where they had just buried Dracula, and he thought he saw something move. Robert shivered. He hurried back into the tent and made his bed.

Alex and Matthew turned their backs to him and pretended to be asleep. Alex made huge snoring sounds.

"Are you all right?" whispered Jared. "I'm sorry they did that."

"I'm fine," said Robert. His toes found some scratchy needles that hadn't fallen out. He searched around for his pillow, but he couldn't find it.

"Hey, do you have my pillow?" Robert asked Jared.

Jared shook his head.

Robert got up from bed and went over to Alex and Matthew's side of the tent. "Give me back my pillow," he insisted.

Alex continued to pretend to snore. Matthew just giggled.

"GIVE IT TO ME!" demanded Robert. He didn't know what he would do if they didn't give it back.

"We don't have it," said Matthew. "We didn't touch it."

"Dracula's probably taking a nap," said Alex.

Robert felt like punching Alex. He was sure that Matthew and Alex had taken his pillow, but he didn't know where they might have hidden it.

"Yeah, Dracula's probably dreaming of monster heaven," said Matthew.

Suddenly Matthew's eyes widened. They all heard a soft howling coming from outside the tent.

"What's that?" asked Alex. He sounded scared.

The howling seemed to get louder.

"Dracula!" whispered Robert in a horrified voice. "He's madder than ever."

"The real Dracula," echoed Jared. "He's here. Haunting the camp. He's not a joke. And he likes young blood. I'm the youngest."

"I'm the second youngest," whispered Matthew in a scared voice. "What if he's coming for me?"

"It's me he wants," said Robert. "I know it. Nothing can stop him."

Just then a bright light shone into the tent. "Boys, it's after lights-out," said Shepard, the tennis counselor who was out on night patrol. "Where's George, your counselor?"

"He went to get some aspirin because his muscles ache," said Matthew.

"All our muscles ache," said Shepard. "Big Robert wants all of his counselors in shape. Anyhow, what's this whispering about?"

"Dracula is out there stalking around," whispered Robert in a scared voice. He knew now that he had done the wrong thing in burying Dracula.

"Maybe Dracula got George," said Matthew. "George has been gone a long time."

"He should be back here," said Shepard. "I'll look for him."

The howling noise grew louder. Even

Shepard looked a little scared. "Now, there's no reason to be scared," he said, but his voice sounded shaky. "Head counselor Robert is out there trying to find the source of the noise."

"We know what's making the noise," said Matthew. "It's Dracula."

Shepard laughed. "Dracula doesn't exist. You've all just been hearing too many ghost stories. Right now, I want this tent to go to sleep. I'll find George and send him back here." Shepard left the tent.

As the flap of the tent blew noisily in the breeze, they all could hear the sound of the howling grow louder and louder.

Robert buried his face in his sheet, wishing he had his baby pillow to hold; but he knew that not even his pillow could save him from Dracula's wrath.

6

Blood Is Thicker Than Water

At breakfast the next morning, Big Robert rang his fork against his glass and called for order. "I know that many of you were kept awake last night by howling. There are usually no wolves in this area, and your counselors and I could find no tracks. Now even if there are wolves, they are not dangerous. Wolves rarely attack humans."

Matthew raised his hand. "What if it isn't wolves, sir?" he asked. "But something more dangerous?"

Big Robert frowned. "What do you mean?"

"What about something superhuman?" Matthew lowered his voice. "Like Dracula."

Big Robert's frown deepened. "Dracula is just a silly story. Enough about this. I just wanted to reassure you that no one is in danger. Now, I will go on with the schedule for the day."

Robert wished that he could believe that no one was in danger, but he knew better. The entire camp was in danger, and it was his fault. Burying the Dracula doll had only made the real Dracula more angry—so angry that he had come and stolen his pillow.

Robert looked across the mess hall. Sam was frantically trying to catch his attention. Robert waved to him. "Meet me outside after breakfast," mouthed Sam.

Robert nodded. He started to eat his blueberry pancakes, normally his favorite food in the world. "Pass the maple syrup," Robert said to Alex.

"Are you sure you don't want some fresh blood?" asked Alex. "Or did you get enough last night? What do you think, Matthew?"

"I think maybe we shouldn't make jokes about Dracula anymore," said Matthew.

"Maybe Dracula had a bad dream," said Alex. "Maybe he missed his soft cushy pillow, right, Matthew?"

Matthew looked down at his plate and didn't answer. Robert pushed the plate of blueberry pancakes away.

Just then George came back to the table, followed by his best friend, Cookie, the cook. They were both smiling and whispering to each other.

"Anything wrong with my pancakes?" asked Cookie.

"No," said Robert. "I'm not hungry."

"Do you have a stomachache?" asked George.

"No," said Robert. "I'm fine."

"In that case," said George with a grin, "do you mind if I finish your pancakes?"

But just as Robert started to hand his plate to George, the head counselor appeared at his shoulder.

"How is your diet, George?" he asked sternly.

"Uh, fine . . . sir," said George.

"And did you jog this morning?" asked Big Robert.

"I was a little stiff from yesterday, sir," said George.

"Nonsense. A good five-mile run will iron the kinks right out."

"Uh, excuse me, sir," interrupted Cookie. "But if we run, we'll go right near the site of the howling . . . and George, here, is not so fast—the wolves might mistake him for a deer and bring him down."

The head counselor did not look amused. "I will not have you make jokes about that confounded noise in front of the young campers. You and George will join me for a five-mile run this afternoon."

Big Robert moved on to another table.

George handed the blueberry pancakes back to Robert. He looked almost as miserable as Robert.

"I'll never make it through the summer," groaned George.

"Me either," said Robert.

"We'll think of something," said Cookie.

Robert asked George if he could be excused, and George let him leave the table. Robert found Sam sitting on the steps of the mess hall waiting for him.

"What took you so long?" asked Sam.

"Big Robert stopped at our table. He wants George to go on a diet."

"I know," said Sam. "He's after all the counselors and campers who are overweight, and both George and Cookie are getting the worst of it. You don't have to worry. You're skinny."

"Being skinny isn't so great," said Robert. "Dracula is supposed to be skinny. Did you hear that howling last night?"

Sam nodded.

"Well, I think Dracula is howling at me," said Robert. "I buried him."

"What!" exclaimed Sam.

Robert told Sam how he and Jared had buried Dracula. "Now my pillow is missing. I think Dracula took it."

"Dracula doesn't exist," said Sam.

"That's easy for you to say," said Robert. "Dracula doesn't hate you."

Just then Billy and another one of Sam's friends came by. "Hey, Bamfords, I know why you stick together," he said.

"Why?" asked Sam.

"Because blood is thicker than water," said Billy.

"Very funny," said Sam.

Robert looked at his brother. "I'm sorry," he said miserably. "You're getting teased because of me."

"It's not you!" said Sam angrily. "Someone is out there pretending to be Dracula, and you're getting blamed. I'm going to catch whoever it is."

Robert shuddered. He imagined Sam sneaking out alone and being caught by the fangs of Dracula himself. "Don't try it," warned Robert.

"I've got to," said Sam. "I'm going out after taps and find the howler."

Robert knew that Sam was stubborn, and that once he decided to do something he almost never changed his mind. "I'll go with you," said Robert. "I got us into it with my stupid pillow."

Sam punched Robert playfully on the arm. "There's nothing to be scared of," he said.

Robert shook his head. He knew better.

7

A Living Nightmare

Robert's feeling of dread grew throughout the day. He barely spoke a word to anyone, even Jared. The gray, drizzly weather did nothing to help Robert's mood. That night, Robert waited several minutes after taps. Then he carefully lifted the edge of the tent nearest his bed and slithered out.

Sam was waiting for him. It was cloudy out, and there was no moon. Suddenly Robert's heart was beating so loud he was sure that Dracula would hear it. Even if by chance they escaped Dracula, Robert knew Big Robert would be furious if he found them.

Suddenly Sam grabbed Robert's arm. "Do you hear something?" he whispered.

In the distance, they could hear a strange low howling sound, almost as if a vampire were whispering.

"It's started," said Sam. "We've got to follow the sound."

"What if it's really Dracula?" whispered Robert.

"Don't be silly," said Sam, but before they could move in the direction of the howling, a low moaning noise came up from the other side of the flagpole.

"There's two of them!" whispered Robert in a terrified voice.

"At least," admitted Sam, listening to a new soft howling noise that seemed to be coming from directly behind the flagpole.

"We're surrounded!" whispered Robert.

"Don't panic," warned Sam.

Robert repeated, "Don't panic," to himself.

High above them they heard the sounds of wings in the trees.

"That's just bats," said Sam calmly. "They're always out at night."

"Bats," groaned Robert.

"They won't hurt you. Outside, they almost never attack."

"Unless they're vampires. Sam, we shouldn't be out here. Please, let's go back," pleaded Robert.

"I'm not going to let a few tiny bats scare me," said Sam.

The clouds parted and the moon came out bright and full, throwing tall shadows from the trees down onto the ground.

"Look!" cried Robert.

Creeping toward the mess hall was a swirling creature dressed in a cape.

"It's him!" screamed Robert, but his scream came out like a strangled whisper. He was too scared even to scream.

But then, just as suddenly as it had appeared, the moon disappeared behind a cloud, throwing everything back into almost total darkness.

"I can't see him anymore," said Sam. He cleared his throat. "Look, I know there's a logical explanation, but I think we'd better get back to our tents. We don't want a counselor to catch us."

"What about Dracula catching us?" asked Robert.

Sam didn't answer the question. "I'll take you back to your tent." Sam grabbed Robert's hand and Robert felt how sweaty Sam's palm was.

As they scurried back to the tent, Robert whispered to Sam, "Now do you believe me that Dracula exists?"

"No," snapped Sam. "We just saw a

weird shadow of a tree."

But Robert knew his brother well, and he knew when Sam was lying.

Robert's blood was pumping so fast he was sure that Dracula could smell it. Sam lifted the tent flap for him. "Hurry," he urged.

"Be careful getting to your own tent," warned Robert.

Sam nodded. He patted Robert on the back. Robert crept into the tent. Everyone seemed asleep. Robert snuck between his sheets. With all his heart, he wished he had his baby pillow, but he knew he had to survive without it. At least he had Sam on his side.

Jared groaned in his sleep. Robert sighed again. Jared was just *having* a nightmare.

Robert felt as if he were *living* one.

8

Does Dracula Have
a Sense of Humor?

The next morning Robert felt great relief when he saw Sam standing with his tentmates at flag raising. At least Sam had made it back in one piece.

The head counselor blew his whistle sharply. "Last night somebody stole a trayful of blueberry muffins and a gallon of ice cream from the mess hall. Furthermore, as I'm sure many of you heard, we were once again treated to that howling noise. I want to make it very clear that I will not tolerate such pranks in my camp."

"Maybe Dracula couldn't get any blood to drink, and he had to eat ice cream," said Cookie in a loud voice.

"Shhh," warned George, but he started to laugh.

"And I don't want to hear any more about Dracula," ordered Big Robert. "I know there have been a lot of Dracula stories circulating around camp, but Dracula is simply a creature of the imagination. The person or people who are wandering around camp stealing food and howling are *not* creatures of the imagination. They are real and they will be caught."

"Is your Dracula doll gaining weight?" asked Alex.

Robert shook his head.

"Say, we haven't seen Dracula in a while," continued Alex. "Hey, Matt, don't you think we should examine the doll to see if he's got a potbelly?"

Matthew laughed weakly.

Robert wished that everyone would stop making jokes about Dracula. He had a dreadful feeling that Dracula did not have a sense of humor. He watched the flag flapping in the cool breeze. He held his hand over his heart and listened to his heartbeat, so steady now. He remembered how it had pounded in the moonlight when he'd seen the shadow of the figure in the cape.

As they trouped into the mess hall for breakfast, Jared tugged at Robert's arm. "I saw you sneak out of our tent last night," he said. "And I didn't tell anyone."

"Thanks," said Robert, leaning closer to Jared. "Sam and I saw the real Dracula last night," he whispered.

Jared stared at him, his eyes so wide they looked huge. "Did he attack you?"

"No," said Robert. "We ran away. Even Sam agreed we had to run."

"Maybe you should tell Big Robert," said Jared.

"What if *he* is Dracula?" asked Robert.

"Well, somebody better do something," said Jared. "The other kids in our tent noticed you were gone too. Alex said that at first he was kidding about you being Dracula, but now he's not so sure. Matthew reminded us about those marks on your neck."

Robert instinctively put his hand on his neck.

"Don't worry," said Jared. "I still don't think you're Dracula."

"Why?" asked Robert.

"I don't know," mumbled Jared. "I guess 'cause I like you, and I don't think I'd like Dracula."

Robert felt so glad that he didn't know what to say.

"Do you want to help Sam and me try to catch Dracula?" asked Robert.

"Why not?" said Jared. "I buried a tiny Dracula. I'm not afraid of a big one."

"I am," admitted Robert.

Jared and Robert didn't have a chance to talk to Sam until both their tents met for archery at eleven in the morning. Robert put on his leather armguard and picked out his bow.

"Robert Bamford," said Alex from a safe distance. "Why do you need a bow and arrow? Your teeth are sharp enough."

Robert tried to ignore him.

"Do you know what Dracula's favorite sport is?" asked Matthew.

"No," said Robert wearily.

"BAT-minton," shouted Matthew. "Don't you get it? Bat . . ."

"I get it," said Robert. "I just don't want it."

"Ignore them," said Jared.

"That's what Sam says," said Robert wearily. "But it's hard."

Robert took his bow and arrow and stood in line next to Sam. "Jared wants to help us," he said.

Sam smiled at Jared. "Thanks, we're going to need help. Somebody is pretending to be Dracula and Robert's getting blamed."

"*Or* Dracula is really here, haunting the camp," said Robert as he drew his bow back and let his arrow go.

"Bull's-eye!" shouted Jared. Robert's arrow hit the exact center of the target.

"I told Jared what we saw last night," said Robert.

"We might have just seen a shadow," said Sam. "It was very dark."

Robert drew out another arrow. He looked very grim. "I'm sure that Dracula is here." He let his arrow go. This time it sailed over the target.

"I'm glad you missed," said Sam. "If you had gotten two bull's-eyes in a row, I would think you were getting help from Dracula."

"This is nothing to joke about," said Robert.

"Robert's right," agreed Jared. "The whole camp may be in danger."

"Hey, Sam," called Sam's counselor. "We're supposed to go to baseball."

Sam turned to Robert and Jared. "I've got to go."

"Hey, Sam," shouted Billy. "Maybe your little brother wants to come. We can always use a BAT boy."

Sam sighed. "We've got to put an end to this. Trust me. I'll think of something."

"I trusted you last night," said Robert, "and we almost got bitten by vampire bats."

Jared shuddered.

9

Operation Garlic

In the free period before dinner, Sam met Robert and Jared behind the arts and crafts tent. "I decided we need to get our hands on some garlic," Sam said.

"I thought *you* didn't believe Dracula was real," said Robert.

"Hold it. . . . I'm not saying I believe in Dracula, exactly, but I've been thinking all day . . . and if, just maybe, Dracula does exist, then I think you might really be in danger. And Mom would kill me if Dracula got you."

"I don't think she'd blame you," said Robert.

"Anyhow, *I* don't want him to get you."

"What are we supposed to do with the garlic?" asked Robert with a sinking feeling.

The fact that Sam now seemed to believe that Dracula could exist scared him more than anything else that had happened.

"You wear it around your neck."

"Yuk, I don't like garlic," said Robert.

"I do," said Jared. "My dad makes great spaghetti sauce with tomatoes and garlic."

"Then you wear it," said Robert.

"It's *you* Dracula wants," insisted Sam.

"I guess we could ask Cookie for some garlic," suggested Jared. "He's nice."

"Even Cookie could be Dracula," said Sam darkly.

"Maybe we could call Mom and ask her to send us some garlic by Express Mail," said Robert.

"It might not get here in time," said Jared. "By then you might already be a vampire."

"I'm not going to turn into a vampire," said Robert.

"You will if Dracula drinks your blood," said Jared.

Sam nodded. Robert wished he didn't look quite so excited by the whole thing. Sam took charge. "We're supposed to have a campfire tonight. While everyone is going to the campfire, we can sneak into the kitchen and get hold of some garlic."

"I don't want to sneak into the kitchen,"

wailed Robert. "If Big Robert catches us stealing garlic, he'll think we stole the other stuff too."

"We won't get caught," insisted Sam. "It'll just take a minute. We'll be back at the campfire before anyone realizes we're not there."

"They'll smell the garlic," complained Robert.

"Better a little smelly than vampired to death," said Jared.

Robert looked up. The counselors were taking their late-afternoon jog around the campsite. Big Robert led the way. Poor George and Cookie brought up the very end. They looked exhausted.

"I got to go," said Sam. "You two meet me under the back porch after dinner."

"I think your brother is neat," said Jared as they watched Sam leave.

"I just hope he knows what he's doing," said Robert.

At dinner, Jared sat next to Robert. They had turkey with gravy. Robert asked for a drumstick.

"I'm glad you like turkey," said George. "I was worried because you weren't eating."

"Of course he likes turkey," said Matthew. "Don't you know what Dracula's favorite holiday is?"

Robert took a bite of his drumstick.

"FANGS-giving," answered Matthew.

"Smile," whispered Jared. "Don't let them know they're getting to you."

"That's what Sam said," whispered Robert.

"Make up a joke back," said Jared. "And keep eating."

Robert took another bite from his drumstick. "Hey, do you know what the boy vampire said to the girl vampire?"

"No. What?" asked Matthew suspiciously.

"I like your blood type," answered Robert.

Jared giggled, and so did George at the head of the table.

Robert began to feel better.

10

Guilty Vampires

"Operation garlic," said Sam when they met him beneath the back porch of the cookhouse. He had a knapsack on his back. In the shadows of the dusk he looked like a hunchbacked dwarf.

"I'll go first," said Sam, acting like a general. He crawled out from under the back porch. Jared and Robert followed him.

Suddenly Sam held up his hand. "Shhh," he warned. "Someone's in the kitchen."

"With Dinah," hummed Robert, thinking of the old railroad song they sang at campfire.

"Shhh . . . I can hear what they're saying," whispered Sam.

"Look, I don't think we should go on with it," argued one voice, quite loudly.

"Just one more night," pleaded another voice. "I agree. We quit after tonight."

"I feel guilty enough as it is," said the other.

"Vampires," whispered Robert. "The vampires are talking to each other."

"I don't think vampires would feel guilty," whispered Jared.

They crouched behind the window. Even Sam wasn't tall enough to see through. "Give me a leg up," he ordered.

Robert and Jared both shook their heads no. "Let's go get Big Robert," said Jared.

"Big Robert could be Dracula," argued Sam. "These could be two vampires he's created."

Robert wished Sam hadn't gotten so into the idea that there were vampires in the cookhouse.

Before they could decide what to do, the kitchen door opened and two creatures flew out. One of them stumbled on the front steps, where Robert was crouched. His cape seemed to swallow up Robert.

"OH, NO! THEY'VE GOT ROBERT!" screamed Jared. "GET SOME GARLIC, QUICK!"

"What do you want garlic for?" asked

the creature with a laugh. His large white fangs gleamed in the moonlight.

"GET AWAY FROM MY BROTHER, DRACULA!" yelled Sam. Fearlessly he charged into the vampire. He grabbed the vampire's fang and it came off in his hand. Sam looked down in amazement. He was holding a plain white drinking straw.

"HEY! YOU'RE NO VAMPIRE," shouted Sam. But the two creatures took off down the path.

"After them!" yelled Sam. He, Robert, and Jared chased after the two creatures. Up ahead, they could see the bright flame from the campfire. The creatures ran awkwardly, trying to cover up their faces with their capes. They weren't very fast, and Sam, Robert, and Jared gained on them.

Sam put on a tremendous burst of speed and caught the cape of one of the vampires. They fell to the ground, and the other creature turned and fell on Sam.

Robert sprinted up the path. He was scared, but he couldn't let Sam fight the creatures alone. Robert jumped on the pile of capes and bodies.

"Help!" cried a voice. "Let us up!"

"Never," said Robert, and he started to punch the vampire he was sitting on. Sam sat on the other one. Jared came huffing up and jumped on too.

"PROTECT YOUR NECK!" yelled Sam. "DON'T LET THEM BITE YOUR NECK!"

"Wait. Nobody wants to bite you," pleaded the creature. "We've got to show them who we are."

The creature unwrapped itself from its cape. It was George. The other creature was Cookie.

"You two are the vampires?" cried Sam.

"At your service," said George.

"Are you really vampires?" asked Robert, trying to keep his neck as far away from Cookie and George as he could.

"No," said George. "You don't have to protect yourselves from us. We were just trying to protect ourselves from Big Robert. He was taking his physical fitness program so seriously, Cookie and I decided to take advantage of all the Dracula jokes flying around camp. We dressed up as Dracula so we could raid the icebox, and Cookie wouldn't get blamed."

"But we felt bad about Robert having to take all the teasing," added Cookie.

"We realized tonight that we were being unfair to you," said George. "Everyone was teasing you for our pranks."

George and Cookie looked at each other. "I think we should go to the campfire," said George. "And confess, even if we get fired."

"I agree," said Cookie. "But don't you think we should dress up for one last grand entrance?"

Robert looked at him doubtfully.

"We didn't mean to hurt you," said George seriously.

"You didn't take my pillow, did you?" asked Robert, in a voice barely above a whisper.

George shook his head. "I didn't realize it was missing."

"Are you still worrying about that baby pillow?" asked Sam.

"Robert's not a baby," said George. "No baby would have had the courage to tackle us. He should get a merit badge for bravery in the face of vampires."

Robert blushed.

"Come on," said Cookie. "Just one last scare for the fun of it. I've got some extra straws in here somewhere."

11

Did Dracula Fool Them All?

They all walked together to the campfire. "Smile," whispered George as they approached the back of the campfire. "And keep behind our capes."

"How can I smile with fangs in my mouth?" whispered Robert. They all had straws sticking from their teeth.

As they walked into the light of the campfire, Big Robert was leading the camp in singing "I Know an Old Lady Who Swallowed a Fly."

Suddenly one of the campers screamed, "Dracula!"

"TWO BIG VAMPIRES AND THREE LITTLE VAMPIRES!" cried another camper.

Big Robert's mouth fell open, and he

stopped singing. George and Cookie walked up to the front of the fire. Then they took off their capes and fangs.

"Dracula does not exist," said George. "Cookie and I have a confession to make. For the past several nights we have been pretending we were Dracula so we could take extra portions of food without anyone noticing. At first I thought it would be a harmless prank, but then I realized that poor Robert Bamford was getting all the blame. It started just because he brought a Dracula doll to camp."

"And a pillow for Dracula to sleep on," added Sam.

"We just wanted to confess, because Robert shouldn't get any more teasing," said Cookie. "Robert and Sam and Jared were very brave tonight. They caught us, and we decided to come to you and take our punishment."

"You certainly are in trouble," said Big Robert.

"Please, sir," said Robert. "Don't be too hard on them. George has been a terrific counselor, and Cookie's a good cook. They just got hungry after all that running."

The head counselor looked down at Robert. "Well, little Robert, I'll take what you say into consideration."

Robert squirmed at the words "little Robert."

Alex and Matthew raised their hands. "We deserve part of the blame, sir," they said. "We started teasing Robert about being Dracula. In fact, we even began to believe that he was Dracula. George tried to make us stop."

"Well," said Big Robert. "Maybe they will not be fired, but I can guarantee you that they will both be doing a lot more running."

George and Cookie groaned.

"Meanwhile," said Big Robert, "I think we should continue our song."

While they were singing, Sam grabbed Robert's hand. "We're heroes," said Sam grinning. "I told you I'd solve everything."

Robert looked around him at the dark woods. He thought he heard a faint howling in the distance. He shivered and told himself it could be just the wind.

As they were getting ready for bed, Matthew climbed onto Robert's bed. "I have my own confession to make," he said.

Robert looked at him.

"I took your pillow. I did it just for a joke, like Cookie and George . . . but then I got scared you might really be Dracula, so I didn't want to tell you."

"Where is it?" asked Robert.

Matthew grinned. "You've been sleeping on it all the time. I hid it in the springs of your cot." Matthew rolled up the corner of Robert's mattress, and there, shoved into the springs, was the pillow.

"I've been sleeping with it and I didn't even know it," said Robert in an awed voice.

"I sleep with my towel," whispered Matthew. "It's sort of like my baby blanket."

Robert looked at his pillow. He was glad to have it back.

The next morning Robert and Jared went to the clearing in the pine trees to dig up Robert's Dracula doll. At first they couldn't find him, and Robert felt a gnawing fear in his stomach. But then he dug into the soft dirt, and he saw something gleaming white. It was Dracula's fang. He dusted Dracula off, and then the fear in his stomach grew.

Dracula seemed to have a smile on his face, a smile that Robert would swear had never been there before. It was as if Dracula knew something that no one else did, as if once again Dracula had fooled them all.